MORE THAN A
PRINCESS

By **Delanda Coleman** & **Terrence Coleman**
Illustrated by **Beatriz Mello**

Cover design and illustrations by Beatriz Mello

Hardback ISBN 978-1-7344158-2-7
Paperback ISBN 978-1-7344158-0-3
eBook ISBN 978-1-7344158-1-0

Library of Congress Control Number : 2019920743

First Edition February 2020

Published by Sydney and Coleman, LLC
www.DelandaColeman.com
Boston, Massachusetts

This book is dedicated to our very own princess, Sydney.

You inspire us every day.
May all your dreams come true.
Love always,
Mom and Dad

Princess Kiana was lying in bed,
"Life in the castle is boring!" she said.

"I've got many things, but I need something more.
There's so much out there I have yet to explore.

"I wish I could find something more I could do."
Then suddenly, someone appeared out of the blue!
Her fairy godmother, oh my what a sight!
She fluttered her wings in elegant flight.

"My darling Kiana, I come from afar
To help you realize just how special you are.

"You wouldn't believe all
the things you can do!
Nothing can stop a smart
Princess like you."

"Well..." said the princess, with a smile on her face,
"I wonder, sometimes, what it's like up in space."

"An astronaut! How exciting!" the fairy replied,
"Follow my lead, and I will be your guide!"

You'll learn about science. You'll study and read.
With practice, you'll get all the skills that you'll need.

"Aboard a space shuttle, you'll zoom through the sky,
And watch the stars twinkle as you're whizzing by."

"On the Space Station, there's no time to rest!
You'll work with your crew and carry out tests.

"Everyone there will be ever so bright,
They'll pilot, fix stuff, even launch satellites!

"You might even be the first princess on Mars,
With passion and work you can reach for the stars!

"You wouldn't believe all the things you can do.
Nothing can stop a smart princess like you!"

Kiana was thrilled, "This trip was such fun!"
"What else would you like to explore, little one?"

"Being a doctor," said Kiana out loud,
"Healing my patients would make me feel proud."

"Great!" said the fairy, "now, follow my lead!"
"Let's see what it's like to help people in need."

The two were now back with their feet on the ground,
...In a room full of doctors, all running around!

The fairy godmother said, "Look at them go!
A day, for a doctor, is never too slow."

"You'll visit your patients and ask how they feel.
You'll do all you can to help all of them heal.

"You'll diagnose and treat. You'll comfort and care,
You'll talk to your patients to make them aware.

"You might wear a stethoscope to listen to hearts,
Or help to fix bones that are broken apart.

"You wouldn't believe all the things you can do.
Nothing can stop a smart princess like you!"

Kiana was excited, "Can we try some more?"
"Of course," said the fairy, "what shall we explore?"

"I'd like to see how engineering is done.
Planning and building sound ever so fun!"

"Good choice!" said the fairy, "Come on now, let's go!
I'll show you the things that you will need to know.

"Engineers can design and devise many things,
From robots and bridges to strong airplane wings.

"You'll choose in which area you should specialize.
You could build new machines that will change people's lives.

"You could help make new highways, long tunnels or roads,
Or design cool computers to decipher codes.

"You could help our great planet become very green,
By making clean energy through new machines."

"You wouldn't believe all the things you can do.
Nothing can stop a smart princess like you!"

"This is so great!" said the princess with a cry.
"So," said the fairy, "what else should we try?"

"Being an artist sounds exciting to me,
I'd love to showcase my art for people to see."

"Ok," said the fairy godmother, "let's start!
Let's see what it takes to make beautiful art.

"There are so many things that artists design:
A product, an advert, a card or a sign.

"You might work with colors of each shade and hue,
Your artwork will show your unique point of view.

princess
kiana
designer

"Your creativity will express what you feel in your heart, Everyone will get lost in your beautiful art.

"They'll come from afar to admire what you've made. Your canvas and prints will be proudly displayed.

by princess Kiama

BUY
$$

TIME
SQUARE

NOW

SALE

LOOK

"You wouldn't believe all the things you can do.
Nothing can stop a smart princess like you!

"But now, we must go, before your parents awake,
Here's my advice that I'd like you to take.

"Work very hard throughout all your years.
Don't get discouraged or stopped by your fears.

Do all your work with great dedication.
Though things might get tough, have no hesitation.

"You wouldn't believe all the things you can do.
Nothing can stop a smart princess like you!

There now was a princess with a vision in hand.
Who knew she'd achieve whatever she planned.

She'd grow to become a princess like no other.
Thanks to the help of her fairy godmother.

ABOUT THE AUTHORS

About Delanda Coleman

Delanda Coleman has spent over a decade as a leader in Product Marketing for some of the world's largest and most innovative software companies. Having seen the fast-paced and evolving nature of technology, she was surprised by the lack of urgency or innovation in recruiting and developing women of color in the software industry. Inspired by the birth of her daughter, she and her husband, Terrence, decided to create Sydney and Coleman Publishing to expose young black girls and boys to concepts and careers in STEAM (science, technology, engineering, art, and math).

A native and resident of Boston, MA, Delanda holds an MBA from New York University and a Bachelors' from Northeastern University. She is an avid reader and world traveler.

You can follow her on Instagram and Twitter @MsDelanda or learn more about her at DelandaColeman.com

About Terrence Coleman

Terrence Coleman is a legal professional in the healthcare industry with a JD from Seattle University School of Law and a Bachelor degree from Rutgers University. Much like his wife, Delanda, Terrence believes that there is a need to inspire children of color to pursue higher-level education. Sydney and Coleman Publishing focuses on promoting and advancing this need.

Terrence was raised in Willingboro, New Jersey and enjoys reading, writing, and physical fitness.

Made in the USA
Monee, IL
21 May 2022

96760843R00019